Going Up

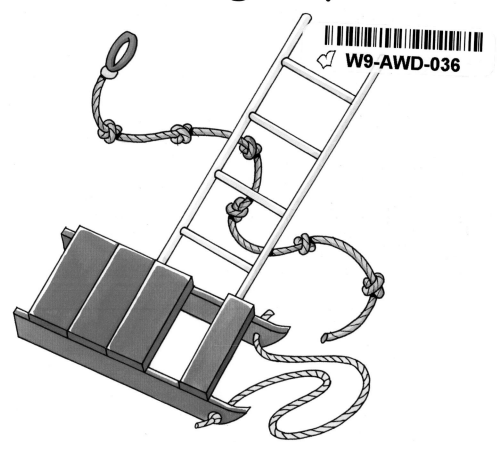

written by Pam Holden
illustrated by Kelvin Hawley

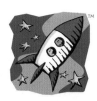

1

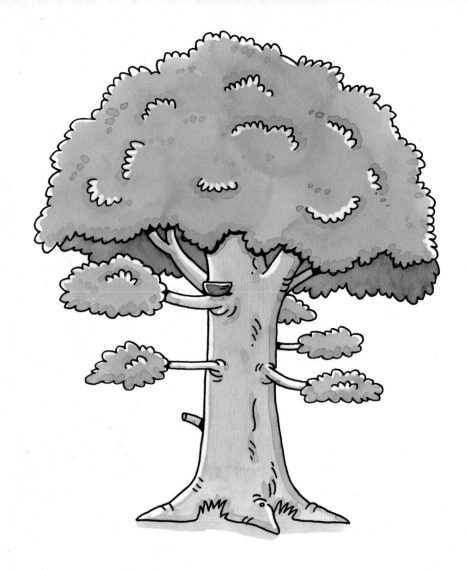

I go up the tree.

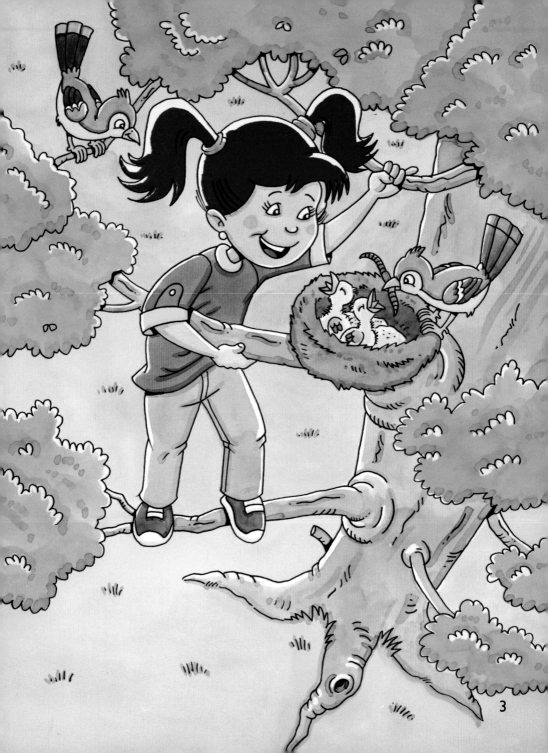

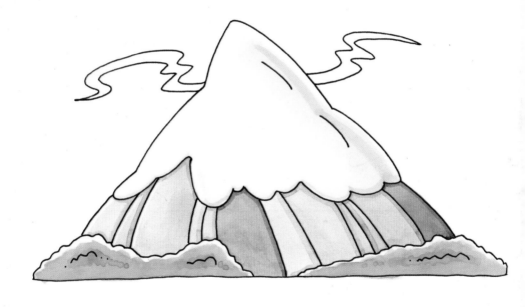

I go up the mountain.

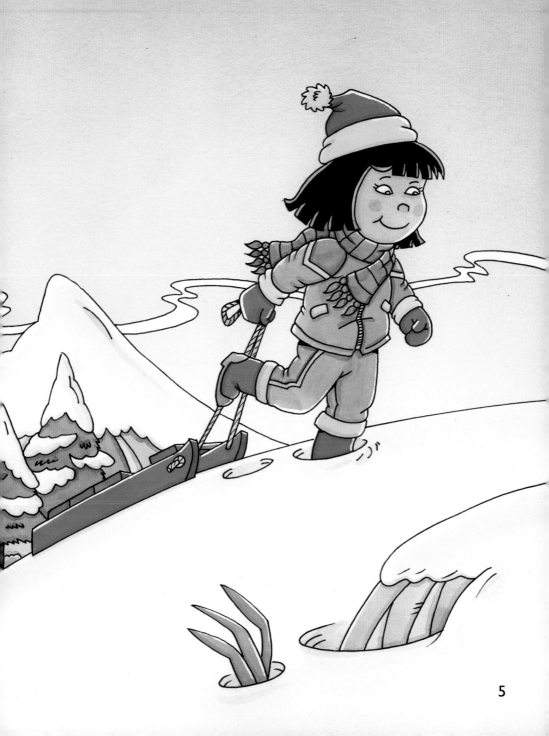

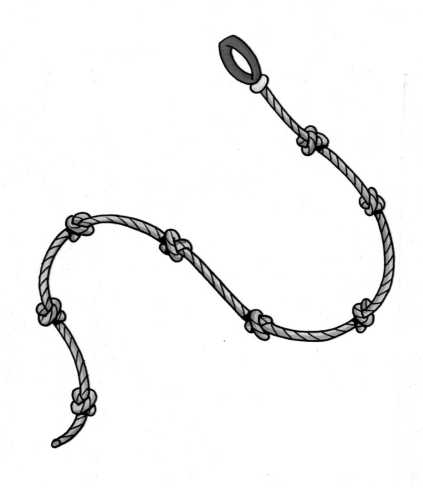

I go up the rope.

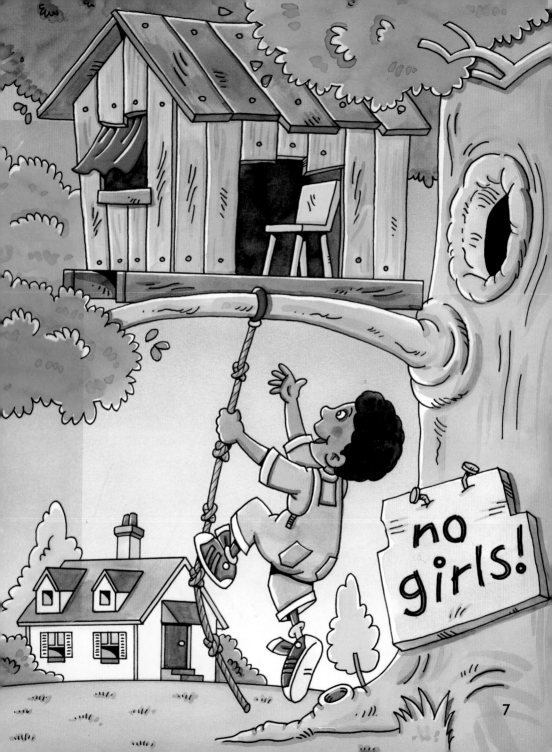

7

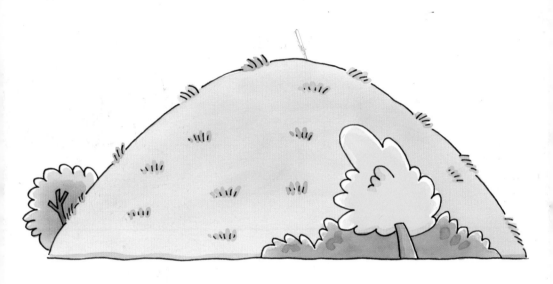

I go up the hill.

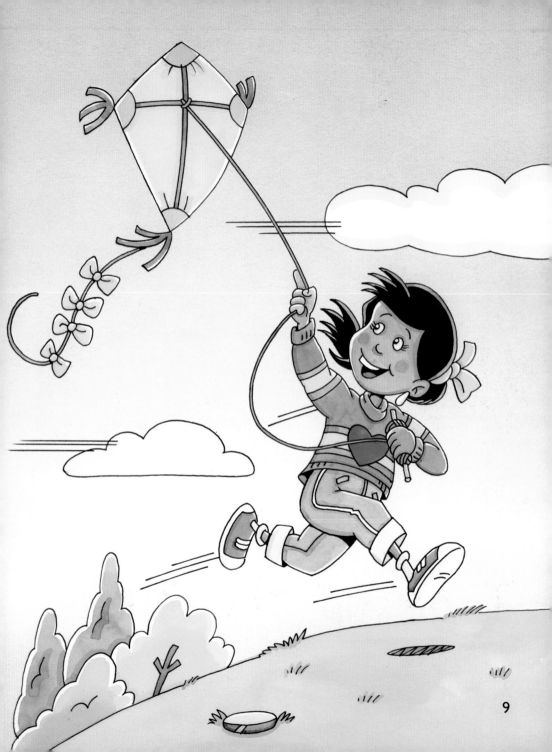

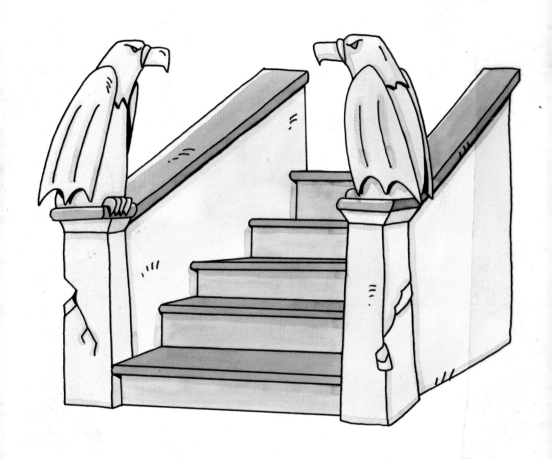

I go up the steps.

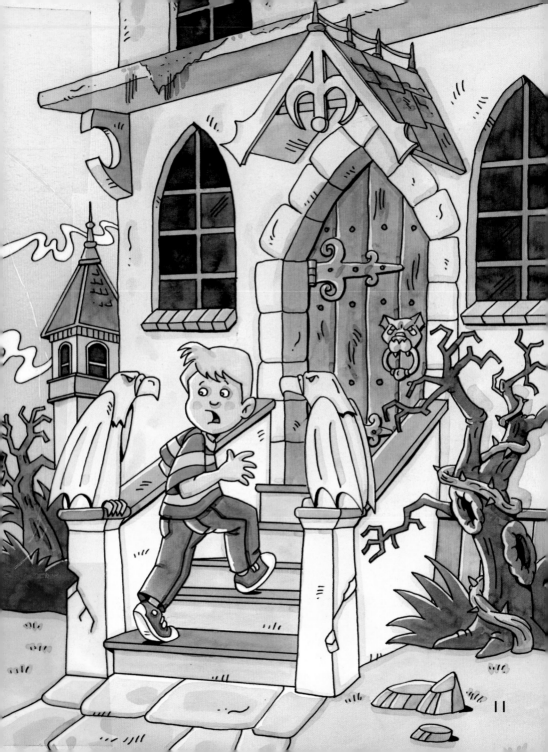

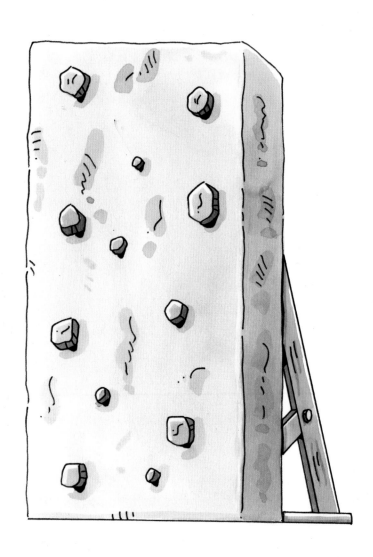

I go up the wall.

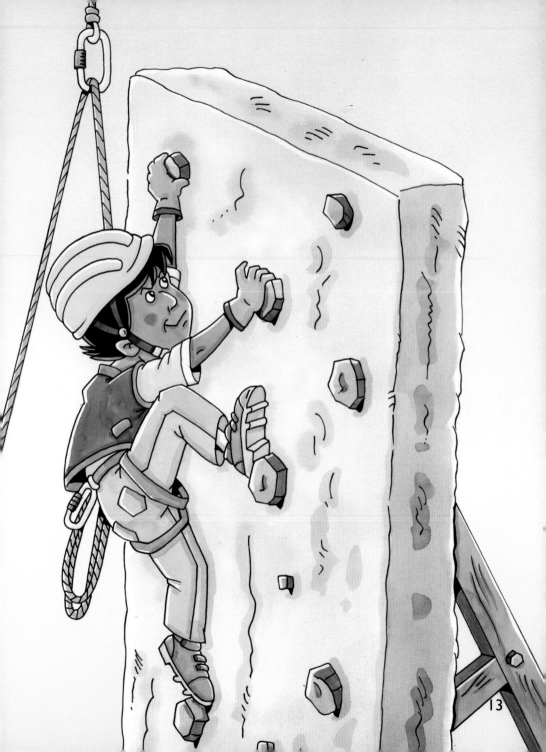

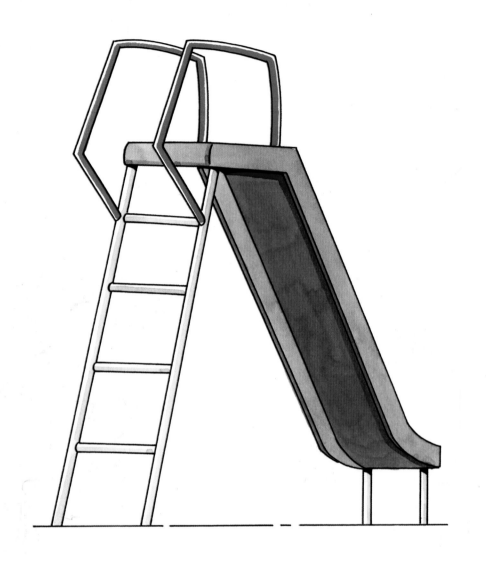

I go up the ladder.

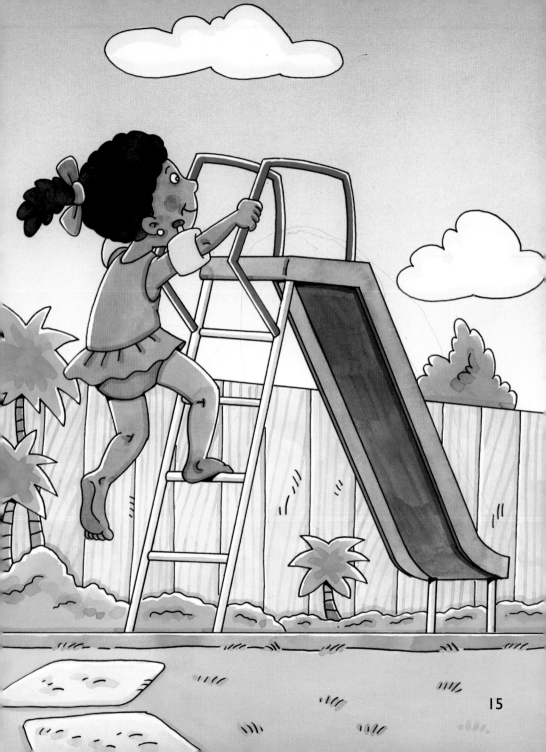

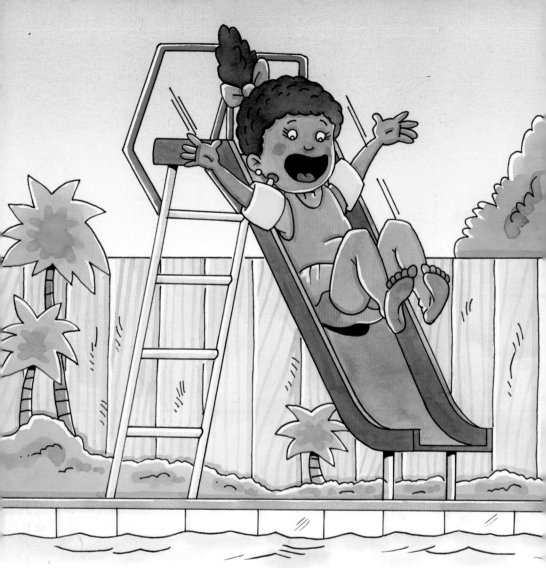

I go down the slide.
Wheee!